1994

Jo- Mandy and Caitlin

Love- Grandma & Grandpa

DADDY LONG EARS' HALLOWEEN

ROBERT KRAUS

LITTLE SIMON
Published by Simon & Schuster Inc., New York

Little Simon
Simon & Schuster Building
Rockefeller Center
1230 Avenue of the Americas
New York, New York 10020

Copyright © 1990 by Robert Kraus

10   9   8   7   6   5   4   3   2   1

ISBN: 0-671-70352-8

Daddy Long Ears' favorite holiday was Halloween.

He liked taking his thirty-two bunnies to choose a pumpkin.

He liked carving the pumpkin into a
Jack-o'-lantern.

He liked making costumes for all the bunnies, and teaching them how to make their own masks.

On Halloween night, Daddy would
take all his bunnies around the
neighborhood Trick-or-Treating.

They were very well behaved and they
never played a trick, even if they didn't
get a treat.

THE OWLS

The Moles

But this Halloween, the youngest of Daddy's bunnies was sick in bed with the flu.

Daddy took his temperature. It was 102!

Daddy called his two eldest sons, Bruce and Billy.

"You'll have to take the bunnies out

Trick-or-Treating this year," he said. "I'm
going to stay home with little Parker."

"Don't worry Daddy," said Bruce and Billy, leading the boys and girls out. "We've watched you all these years, and we know just what to do."

THE
LONG
EARS

Daddy carried Parker downstairs

and made a bed for him on the couch.

Suddenly, there was a knocking at the front door. It was the little foxes, Trick-or-Treating.

Next came the little bear cubs.
"What fun," said little Parker.

"Meow."
"Meow."
"Meow."
said the three little kittens.
"Meow to you, too,"
laughed little Parker.

The next time Daddy opened the door, some little snakes dashed in, sprayed Daddy and Parker with whipped cream, stole all the treats, and ran away before you could say "Jack Rabbit!"

"We'll be ready for the next tricksters,"
said Daddy.

He got two spray cans of whipped
cream, and he and Parker waited.
Suddenly, there was a knock at the door!

Daddy opened the door, and he and
Parker sprayed—Bruce and Billy!

"I'm sorry," said Parker. "Me, too," said Daddy.

"Don't worry," said Bruce and Billy. "What's Halloween without a trick or two?"

All the other bunnies shared their treats
with Parker and Daddy Long Ears.

"This is the best Halloween in my
entire life!" said little Parker—and
they all agreed.

THE END